Editor: Nadia Higgins
Designer: John Moldstad
Page production: Picture Window Books
The illustrations in this book were prepared digitally.

Picture Window Books
5115 Excelsior Boulevard
Suite 232
Minneapolis, MN 55416
1-877-845-8392
www.picturewindowbooks.com

Printed in the United States of America.

Library of Congress Cataloging-in-Publication Data
Dahl, Michael.
Dino rib ticklers : hugely funny jokes about dinosaurs /
written by Michael Dahl ; illustrated by Brandon Reibeling.
p. cm. — (Read-it! joke books)
Summary: An easy-to-read collection of jokes about raptors,
triceratops, and other dinosaurs.
ISBN 1-4048-0122-7 (library binding)
1. Dinosaurs—Juvenile humor. 2. Wit and humor, Juvenile.
[1. Dinosaurs—Humor. 2. Riddles. 3. Jokes.]
I. Reibeling, Brandon, ill. II. Title. III. Series.
PN6231.D65 D34 2003
818'.5402—dc21
                                                    2002156399

A Note to Parents and Caregivers:

Read-it! Joke Books are for children who are moving ahead on the amazing road to reading. These fun books support the acquisition and extension of reading skills as well as a love of books.

Published by the same company that produces *Read-it!* Readers, these books introduce the question/answer pattern that helps children expand their thinking about language structure and book formats.

When sharing a book with your child, read in short stretches, pausing often to talk about the pictures and the meaning of the book. The question/answer format works well for this purpose and provides an opportunity to talk about the language and meaning of the jokes. Have your child turn the pages and point to the pictures and familiar words. Read the story in a natural voice; have fun creating the voices of characters or emphasizing some important words. And be sure to re-read favorite parts.

There is no right or wrong way to share books with children. Find time to read with your child and pass on the legacy of literacy.

Adria F. Klein, Ph.D.
Professor Emeritus
California State University
San Bernardino, California

Look for the other books in this series:
Animal Quack-Ups: Foolish and Funny Jokes About Animals (1-4048-0125-1)
Chewy Chuckles: Deliciously Funny Jokes About Food (1-4048-0124-3)
Galactic Giggles: Far-Out and Funny Jokes About Outer Space (1-4048-0126-X)
Monster Laughs: Frightfully Funny Jokes About Monsters (1-4048-0123-5)
School Buzz: Classy and Funny Jokes About School (1-4048-0121-9)

Dino
Rib
Ticklers

Hugely Funny Jokes About Dinosaurs

Michael Dahl • Illustrated by Brandon Reibeling

Reading Advisers:
Adria F. Klein, Ph.D.
Professor Emeritus, California State University
San Bernardino, California

Susan Kesselring, M.A., Literacy Educator
Rosemount-Apple Valley-Eagan (Minnesota) School District

PICTURE WINDOW BOOKS
Minneapolis, Minnesota

What do you call a dinosaur who steps on a car?

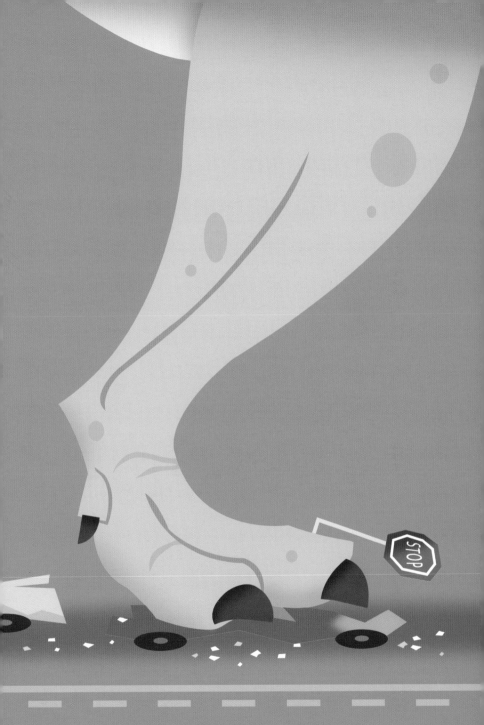

Tyrannosaurus wrecks.

Why did the dinosaur cross the road?

It was the
chicken's day off.

What toys do dinosaurs play with?

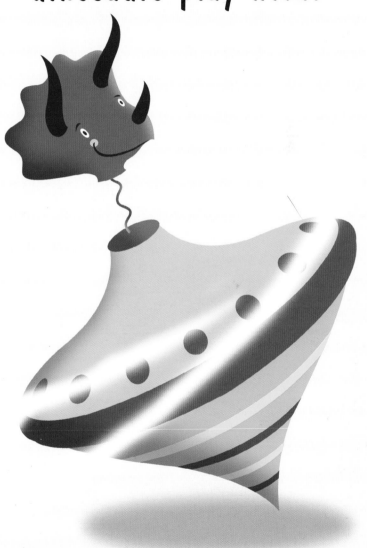

Tricera-tops.

What do you call a dinosaur stuck in a glacier?

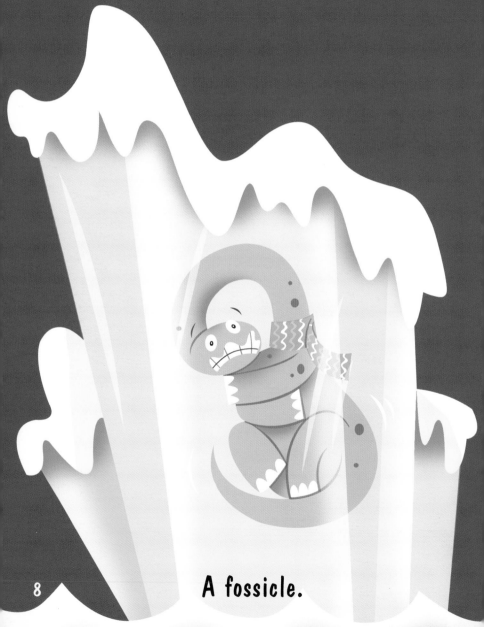

A fossicle.

Who is the fastest dinosaur?

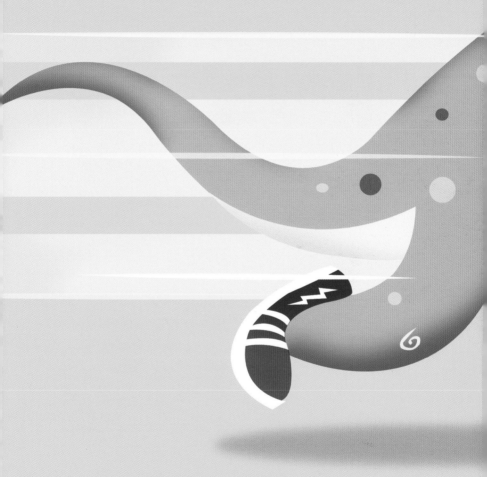

A Prontosaurus.

What kind of music do dinosaurs make?

Rock.

What do you get when you cross a Stegosaurus with a pig?

A porky-spine.

What sport does a T. rex like to play?

Squash!

What day of the week do Raptors eat their food?

Chewsday.

Where was the Ultrasaurus when the sun set?

In the dark.

Why do museums display old dinosaur bones?

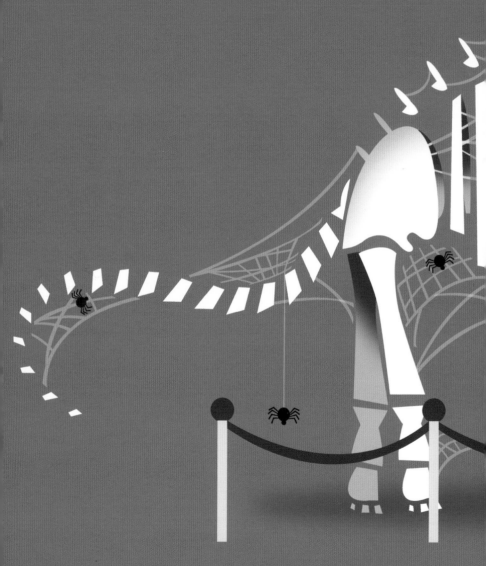

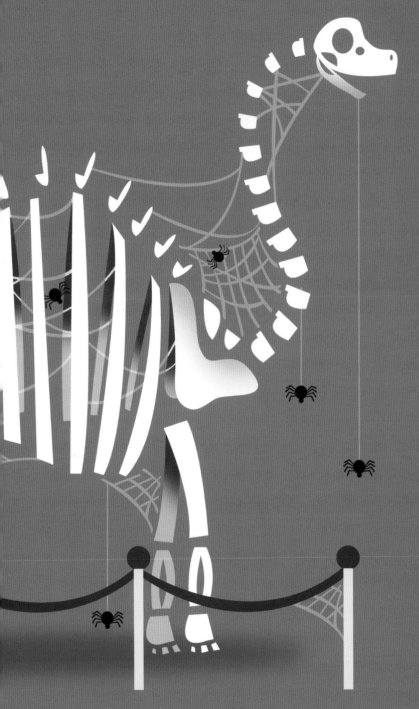

They can't afford new ones.

Where does a Triceratops sit?

On its Tricera-bottom.

What makes more noise than a dinosaur?

Ten dinosaurs!

What do you call a dinosaur that talks and talks and talks?

Blah Blah Blah...

A dino-bore.

Where does a Dimetrodon find its dinner?

At the dino-store. 21

How do you make a dinosaur float?

Take one dinosaur, add root beer
and three scoops of ice cream.   23

What's bigger than a dinosaur but doesn't weigh anything?

A dinosaur's shadow.